CONTENTS

Title Page	2
Prelude	4
Chapter 1: Bartender Zeus Saves the Gods	5
Chapter 2: Poseidon Makes the Best Smoothies	8
Chapter 3: Join the Treat Hades Better Club, No Initiation Fee	12
Chapter 4: Demeter, Proud Goddess of Lucky Charms	16
Chapter 5: Hera Can't Teach an Old Dog New Tricks	19
Chapter 6: #Hestia/Out #Dionysus/In	23
Chapter 7: Apollo is Sizzling Hot (No, Literally)	27
Chapter 8: Artemis has a Girls-Only Club	31
Chapter 9: Athena Breaks the Headline (That is Zeus' Headline)	35
Chapter 10: Aphrodite is Snow White 2.0	40
Chapter 11: Hephaestus Puts His Mom in	45

Timeout

Chapter 12: Is the Word NightmARES, Originated from Ares?   49

Chapter 13: Hermes, the Turtle and the Cow   54

Chapter 14: The Olympian Gods' Intertwined Family   60

About the Author   63

Greek Gods
For Kids

Shaya Dadmehr

PRELUDE

Welcome! In this book, you're probably expecting to read boring mythology stories because your parents forced you to. You're not alone, I feel you, (I'm 10-years-old). Well don't worry, I'm not totally boring, I think I'm funny... my friends don't, but I think I'm funny. Yeah, I have a good sense of humor, "good-job-me" *pats myself on the back*. In this book, I will tell you about these boring Greek mythologies on the major Olympian gods and goddesses. Hope you enjoy (prove your parents wrong and actually enjoy it!)

CHAPTER 1: BARTENDER ZEUS SAVES THE GODS

Zeus didn't have the most pleasant childhood. Once he was born, his mother, Rhea, hid him from his father, Cronus, who was planning to have Zeus as a snack. I'm not joking, Cronus decided to eat Zeus, because of a prophecy (a prediction) that one of his children would dethrone him and take his place. His solution to that was... LET'S EAT 'EM! His wife, Rhea, was fed up with Cronus eating their other kids, yes, he ate 5 other gods/goddesses which were Zeus' siblings, starring Hera, Hestia, Hades, Poseidon and Demeter. CANNIBALISM! Back to the point, as a kid, Zeus had a tough time surviving. His mother Rhea hid him away and gave him to nymphs, female spirits of the natural world, and satyrs, half goat men, to take care of him and train him to fight. Apologies if I just gave you the image of a nymph in a kung-fu stance, getting ready to fight. You're probably wondering, didn't Cronus know about Zeus' existence? Yes, he actually did, amazing right, I thought he was too dumb when he thought of the solution...LET'S EAT 'EM! But Rhea outsmarted Cronus by swapping Zeus with a rock...good job, one-point Rhea on problem-solving, Cronus zero.

Let's fast forward, when Zeus was old enough, he stole Cronus' throne by becoming his bartender. Zeus' plan was to make Cronus trust him by serving him drinks, and it worked! Believe me, it's true, I couldn't make this stuff up in my wildest dreams. So this is how it went down: during a big drinking contest, at a feast with all the Titans (children of Uranus (Heaven/Sky) and Gaia (Earth) and their descendants), Zeus poisoned Cronus' drink causing Cronus to barf out Zeus' siblings who then all united and prepared for war against the Titans and their cannibalistic father. I bet you know who won. Yes, the good guys or shall I say, the "good gods" won and dethroned Cronus and tossed him and all the other Titans in Tartarus (a black hole used as a dungeon to retain and torment evildoers, a.k.a. hell for Titans). All of Cronus' kids became powerful gods/goddesses, with Zeus being the youngest and most powerful. Moral of the story, parents treat your kids right; otherwise, you don't know what's in store for you when they grow up.

Now, if you're having an outdoor party and bad weather strikes, I feel for you, but you know whose fault it is; if you don't know, it's Zeus'. The chapter is all about him, look at the title. Do you know why it's Zeus' fault? It's his fault because he is the god of the sky and thunder. Zeus is said to have lightning bolts that are so powerful they can knock down any monster or object. You shouldn't worry about getting struck by lightning though, Zeus only throws his lightning bolts at people who (1) betray him, (2) do something extremely bad, or (3) just straight up annoy him. Like if you (1) stole something from him, (2) if you're disrespectful in his temples or shrines or (3) if you're just plain old annoying. Number 3 is the most common, just kidding, I just wanted to wake you up, did it work? See I told you I'm funny (if you don't know what's going on and you think I'm crazy, read the prelude).

CHAPTER 2: POSEIDON MAKES THE BEST SMOOTHIES

Being Poseidon you have many choices, am I making this sound like a fast food commercial with endless $1 options? Sorry, let's get back to the point; what I mean is Poseidon can do an array of things. He's versatile, because he's the god of the sea. Being the god of the sea, he can technically create almost any natural disaster that his heart desires, tsunami ✓, hurricane ✓, tidal wave ✓, really appetizing smoothies that are to die for ✓, and earthquakes ✓. How you ask? Well, the earth is surrounded by water. If someone got him in a livid mood, he could even drown whole cities. Wow! That was the most educational thing, I wrote in this entire book so far, "Mommy are you proud of me?" "Yes sweetie, I'm very proud." I'm not sure if that was sarcasm or not; probably was.

Shaya Dadmehr

As cool as it sounds, a surfer god surrounded by pretty mermaids, being Poseidon wasn't all peaches and cream, being Poseidon, you had to get used to the "middle child syndrome." Poseidon was always told, "you're almost as strong as Zeus" or "you're not as conniving as Hades." So, being Poseidon you had to get used to being the meat in the hamburger bun from McDonalds. I just had to insert McDonalds in this book with its golden arches, fit for gods, it's just necessary. I think it's past my dinner time; I can't stop thinking of food.

On a serious note, did you know Poseidon created horses? No not seahorses, but actual horses. The reason he created horses was because he wanted to marry Demeter, the goddess of agriculture, crops and harvest. We'll discuss Demeter later and if you were paying attention you would know Demeter, Poseidon, Zeus, Hades, Hera and Hestia are all siblings who threw their father Cronus in Tartarus...and yes gods and goddesses can marry each other even if they are siblings. By definition, almost all gods and goddesses are related. If you still don't understand this concept, talk to your parents and make them feel a bit uncomfortable...payback for making you read this book 😊. Back to the story, the conversation went something like this, "Hi sis, I want to marry you, do you want to marry me?" She then gibbered, "absolutely not, why would I want to marry someone like you, but if you make the prettiest animal on earth, I'd like that." So, he then created horses, even though I've seen some not-so-pretty horses like some really-hard-on-the-eyes horses; some you hope never to see...I don't know how I managed to say that in three different ways, but I did. Anyway, Demeter never did marry Poseidon, but you've got to give him an "A" for effort...I don't know why my mom always recites this saying, "hello...effort doesn't start with an *A*!!!??"

Another story about Poseidon is what I like to call "The Trojans," doesn't it have an evil undertone? Okay so I may be a bit biased on this one, as my parents are both UCLA alumni, "Go Bruins, Fight, Fight, Fight!" Back to the story, Hera, Poseidon's sister and the goddess of marriage and family, decided to seek revenge against Zeus, who was their brother and Hera's husband, for marrying a woman, because she was promised that she would be Zeus' one and only wife. Hera recruited Poseidon alongside Apollo, the sun god, and Zeus' son from another goddess (it's not the first time Zeus broke his promise to Hera), and Athena, the goddess of wisdom, and Zeus' daughter born from Zeus' head...I warned you these Greek gods and goddesses are all related, it makes my head spin trying to explain their relations to one another. Back to the story, Poseidon didn't want to betray Zeus and get on his brother's bad side, but he finally agreed, reluctantly and halfheartedly. When the two gods and goddess were caught red handed by Zeus, Apollo and Poseidon were punished; while, Athena dodged punishment, it helps to be the smart one out of the group. Poseidon's punishment was to build a wall for the city of Troy while his powers were stripped away after being turned into a mortal. Luckily though, he was promised wages for his assiduous work. When Poseidon finally completed building the wall, he wasn't paid the wages he was promised, the king, Laomedon, claimed "your payment is your godly powers." Poseidon was livid, so in the Trojan war, Poseidon sided with the Greeks. Since he was still fuming, Poseidon sent the wrath of a sponge named Bob upon the Trojans, and that's how SpongeBob got his start! Just kidding, he actually sent a sea monster that loudly hollered "RAAAAAAAAR!" and then let out a gigantic flood killing many souls. Just to make myself feel better and so I don't think about the lives perished, I imagine the sea monster farting out of the water with a big awkward flaming hot face, it really makes me feel better, try it yourself. It's also crucial to act out the sea monster role in front of family members during the least opportune times to break up the monotony of boring family gatherings and to make yourself feel alive.

CHAPTER 3: JOIN THE TREAT HADES BETTER CLUB, NO INITIATION FEE

Hades is probably the unluckiest god ever. People believe he has no soul, because he is the god of the underworld and death, but I don't think that's a fair representation, so please join me in the "Treat Hades Better" club, a.k.a. "THB" club. One thing that bothers me is whenever I ask people to join me in the THB club, they seem to always say "sorry, I'm too busy playing video games." I don't know if that's a "yes" or "no", it's a pretty simple question, don't you think? Hades is the least lucky because when the big three gods (Zeus, Poseidon and Hades), were rolling the dice to see who gets what part of the world, Hades got the last pick. Since he was so lonely and miserable, his Roman name became "Pluto" meaning ruling all that is, "below the surface." Side note, Greek and Roman gods are essentially the same with different names. If you're interested to learn more, do some research and make your parents proud.

Another matter that has bothered me and that I've never understood is why people say Hades is the least strong out of the big three (Zeus, Poseidon, and Hades)? I think he may be the strongest because he can easily and effortlessly create a zombie apocalypse. If he dislikes a mortal, he can send them to the fields of punishment (a.k.a. hell), and just his personality, in general, is extremely sneaky and conniving.

Hades' sneaky and conniving personality coupled by his extreme loneliness shine through when he decides it's time to have a companion in the underworld and kidnaps and hoodwinks his niece Persephone (Demeter and Zeus' daughter) to become his wife; there totally won't be any consequences...I guess the apple doesn't fall far from the tree? He's almost as brainless as his dad, Cronus, who decided to eat his kids to prevent a prophecy from occurring. We witnessed how that worked out: how is it in Tartarus, Cronus? Okay let's not get sidetracked, this is how it all went down. When Persephone was frolicking in the flowers like a bunny, Hades decided to sprout up from the ground like an unwanted weed and snatch her up. Demeter, not being able to find her daughter, went crazy. Since Demeter was so stressed out, all the crops started

Greek Gods for Kids

withering away. The crops were probably having a conversation somewhat like this, "Herb, do you think In-n-Out got her order wrong?" "Maybe that's what happened, Ginger?" "We must die now; otherwise, she'll kill us in a more painful way when she finds us!" "Yeah, you're right, we must die now."

Unbeknownst to her, Persephone wasn't allowed to eat anything in the underworld because if she did, she would be considered "attached there" and would have to remain in the underground for part of the year. Since Hades knew this, he set to accomplish the task at hand. When he was giving Persephone a tour of his garden, yes, he has a garden in the underworld where everyone dies (that's some common sense there, right?). Anyway, when Hades was giving Persephone a tour of his underground garden, a dead soul watering the plants, innocently offered Persephone a pomegranate. She couldn't resist the offer and ate the mouthwatering juicy pomegranate, without hesitation. After Demeter checked everywhere except the underworld, she knew where to find Persephone. Demeter recruited Hermes, the god of thievery and travel and the son of Zeus (a.k.a. Persephone's half-brother and Demeter's and Hades' nephew) to find her daughter. Once Hermes located Persephone, he asked her one question, "Did you eat anything in the underground?" The toothless dead soul with a sly grin, instructed her to "show Hermes her blood-stained hands." Since Persephone ate in the underworld,

Shaya Dadmehr

Winter was created. Legend has it there are no crops in the Winter because Persephone is held in the underworld during the Winter months with Hades and Demeter is always heartbroken during the season, so all the crops have the same conversation, they had earlier in the chapter, "we must die now". So please join the THB club now. Hey, don't judge, what would you do if no one wanted to hang out with you and you were super lonely? And look on the bright side...Winter Vacation, NO SCHOOL!!!

CHAPTER 4: DEMETER, PROUD GODDESS OF LUCKY CHARMS

Hey, Demeter isn't all that manic, depressing and monotonous as depicted in the last chapter... she's the goddess of agriculture, crops, farming and Lucky Charms. Think about it, without crops, we would all be in the underworld with Persephone and Hades. I'm predicting Demeter became the goddess of agriculture because of her childhood experience when her father, Cronus, swallowed her and her siblings whole, as explained in the Zeus Chapter, and in order to prevent cannibalism from becoming a trend, Demeter desired to provide plenty of food for all creatures. Enough of my astute predictions and now moving on to the facts: Demeter was a kind and pretty goddess with a hidden temper (i.e. creating Winter, as explained in the last chapter). It was her kindness, beauty, and ability to feed the masses, not her hot temper that had many gods proposing to her at one point or another. After all, they say the way to a man's heart is through his stomach.

One of Demeter's most infamous marriage proposals was crafted by Zeus. This is how it started: Demeter was in her patch of wheat, eating Lucky Charms when Zeus casually came rocketing down from the sky and announced, "Hey sis, do you want to marry me and have kids?" Demeter had the same response as in the Poseidon Chapter and replied with a firm "NO!" While Zeus kept blabbering about how great it would be to have kids and how powerful s/he would be, Demeter was thinking of an escape plan. Since, Demeter could transform into various animals, she transformed into a snake and slithered away.

Oh, my goddess, I mean; oh my goodness, what a smart plan, PSYCHE! Zeus, being the most powerful Greek god, could obviously also transform into a snake. In a flash, Zeus too, slithered after Demeter. Wasn't that such a dumb decision on Demeter's part? Oh, it gets worse! Since, Demeter ate too many Lucky Charms and already used up her three wishes, she slithered down a dark hole, with nowhere to go. Being the king of the gods, Zeus had no one to answer to and plenty of time on his hands, so he blocked the entrance of the hole and waited. A minute passed, an hour passed, a day passed, a week passed, a month passed, several months passed, until Demeter finally surrendered and agreed to have a child with Zeus.

Demeter, next time, use your brain! Summon your sister, Hera, she'll take care of business; all you need to say is, "Your husband, Zeus, is flirting with me." Zeus' and Demeter's child was Persephone and I predict Demeter is glad she had a child with Zeus because it's obvious Persephone is her favorite offspring, evident by Demeter being extremely livid when Persephone went missing, which was explained in the Hades Chapter.

Next time you're in a gardening class and bored out of your mind, think about how ballistic Demeter became, creating Winter and all, when Persephone went missing. Also remember during gardening class, without Demeter there would be no plants, without plants there would be no animals, and without plants and animals, you would cease to exist. I know, and to think gardening class is a life and death situation...mind blowing, right, so as originally stated, Demeter isn't all that manic, depressing and monotonous after all.

CHAPTER 5: HERA CAN'T TEACH AN OLD DOG NEW TRICKS

Hera is the goddess of women, marriage, family, and childbirth, so you can thank her for being born and having a family to call your own. Hera is also revered as the protector of women, which is ironic as Hera is best known for taking her anger out on the many females her husband/brother Zeus courts. I guess you could say, when it comes to Zeus, Hera never learned the saying "you can't teach an old dog new tricks." For the sake of time in this chapter, we will explore Zeus' involvement with the North African Libyan queen, Lamia, where Hera's hatred was deeply rooted, but rest assured in this book, you will learn about many stories of what I'd like to refer to as the "**3Rs**"…Hera's **R**age, **R**evenge and **R**uthlessness.

The story of Semele, Dionysus' mom, will be

Greek Gods for Kids

covered in chapter 6, the story of Leto, Apollo and Artemis' mom in chapter 7, the story of Hercules' madness, which was onset by Hera in chapter 12, and the story of Maia, Hermes' mom in Chapter 13. There is a cliché that states, "You can be the moon and still be jealous of the stars"; unfortunately, that seems to be true in Hera's case. Although Hera's the queen of the gods and her husband Zeus is the king of the gods, she's still extremely jealous of less powerful females that are romantically involved with her husband. I guess being the goddess of marriage and family, Hera's blood boils when Zeus doesn't take the vows of their marriage seriously.

Now let's dive into the story of Lamia, the Libyan queen, and Zeus' romantic rendezvous. Zeus was performing his daily hobbies, marrying goddesses, queens and princesses when he stumbled upon the queen of Libya, named Lamia. I'm going to get those two words mixed up. Lamia was Poseidon and Lybie's daughter...why so many Ls!!??? Anyway, to recap, Zeus was having a relationship with the Libyan queen, named Lamia, whose mother's name was Lybie. Deja vu, this is sounding like "The Woman Who Swallowed a Fly" song.

As a side note and as you will read in later chapters, Hera, being the goddess of marriage, finds out about every marriage Zeus enters when he'd promised to marry none other than Hera. However, out of all the stories depicting Hera's **3Rs**, this story gave me the biggest chills with chattering teeth action. Now it might have been the ice cream I was eating at the time, but beware this story may give you the heebie-jeebies.

Hera waited to seek vengeance as Zeus and Lamia were expecting the delivery of their newborn. Unbeknownst to them, Hera, being the goddess of childbirth, knew of this news months in advance, so she had time to devise the most revolting, repellent, and repulsive plan (not to be confused with the original **3Rs**). It all unfolded when Zeus and Lamia had just delivered their baby, oh yay what a joyous moment: NOT…Hera, without hesitation, killed the child. Meet Hera, the goddess of FAMILY and CHILDBIRTH. Hera you just killed an innocent newborn demigod (one parent human/mortal, Lamia, and the other a god/immortal, Zeus). Oh, but it gets worse! Lamia had more babies, but now, Hera forced Lamia to kill her own newborns. Okay, that's too disturbing; I need more ice cream to soothe my nerves! Hera's wrath continues; however, after some time, Hera got bored of Lamia killing her own children, so she transformed Lamia into a child eating demon, causing her to steal other people's children and have them for lunch (more cannibalism)…isn't there a Burger King or Dairy Queen in your Libyan palace?

Lamia was so feared by kids around the world that for generations, parents would threaten their kids, saying "If you go to sleep one-minute past 8:00 pm, Lamia the queen of Libya the daughter of Lybie (a.k.a. the boogey-monster) will eat you." Come to think of it, when I was little, my mom would get me to obey her every command by saying "The raccoon will come," as there was a raccoon that would visit our back yard and it scared the daylights out of me. Mom, Lamia the queen of Libya the daughter of Lybie (a.k.a. the boogey-monster) would have been much more effective; although, it would probably cost you a lot in therapy bills if you did threaten me with the boogey-monster. Anyway, this story proves that Hera should not be the goddess of family and childbirth and in chapter 11 of this book, I will prove my point even further. I'm petitioning to recruit myself as a Greek god so I can restore balance, justice, and peace around the world and on Mount Olympus where the Olympian Gods reside...no I don't want to be the god of love, peace, and happiness, I'd prefer to be the god of wealth, pleeeeease!

CHAPTER 6: #HESTIA/ OUT #DIONYSUS/IN

Unlike Hera, Hestia's one of the more peaceful gods who won't tear you to shreds if you raised your arm up for a high five and swiped it down and yelled "PSYCHE!" She'd probably just laugh alongside with you; but don't test it out... no guarantees. She was the first child of Cronus and Rhea, and the first to be gulped down by her daddy. Maybe all that meditation she did in her dad's tummy before being regurgitated is what has made her such a warm, kind, and generous goddess; although, my mom claims it's because she never got married, which is the secret recipe for patience and more patience. She's known as the maiden goddess of the hearth, architecture, domesticity, family, and the state. If you've read Greek mythology before, you probably don't know Hestia as well as other gods/goddesses, because she's no longer one of the main Olympians. Don't get ahead of yourself, there's no #SCANDAL; the reason for her departure and abdication was onset by all the other gods/goddesses #SCANDALS. Although Hestia left the council and chose to give up her seat to Dionysus, she still resides on Mount Olympus.

Honestly, Hestia is a pretty boring goddess, so let's talk about the creation of Dionysus...#REAL SCANDAL. Dionysus was the son of Zeus and the Theban princess, Semele. As we know from the previous chapter, Hera unveils every relationship Zeus has with other females. Hera was obviously devising an evil plan to ruin poor Semele's life. Hera had it all mapped out, Zeus had divulged his identity to Semele, but never appeared in front of her in his divine form, since human beings will disintegrate in the presence of a god's natural form. Nonetheless, Hera's **3Rs** sprang into action and she put her ungodly plan into motion. While Semele was pregnant with Dionysus, Hera disguised herself as a benevolent woman and befriended Semele, telling her, "You should tell your husband that if he's really the mighty Zeus, the god of the sky, he should prove his devotion and love by showing you his original form." Semele thought this was a magnificent idea and a great way to bond with Zeus.

Semele was probably delusional from all the kicking the baby was doing to her insides, because she should've known seeing Zeus in his true form would surely kill her. Nonetheless, Semele demanded repeatedly that Zeus prove his love and show his true form. Zeus adamantly refused, but Semele kept persisting, until she wore out Zeus and he reluctantly agreed. As expected, Semele was disintegrated instantaneously, but her baby, Dionysus, was miraculously unharmed. I guess what doesn't kill you, only makes you stronger. Zeus, knowing Hera would come after Dionysus next, sewed Dionysus into his thigh until the coast was clear. Quick question, don't babies need food? Anyway, somehow from feeding off of god blood, Dionysus turned into a god. Yeah if that's the only way to become a god, I'll pass. Wait, come to think of it, that's not much different than being in your mother's womb, right? Never mind, I changed my mind, I still want to be the god of wealth. Anyway, the moral of the story is; don't ever view a god in their divine form unless you want to combust like the 4th of July fireworks.

Dionysus is the only Olympian with a mortal parent. There is Hercules, but he isn't an Olympian god. Due to his demigod pedigree, Dionysus is considered an outcast and looked down upon by the other gods...no wonder there is so much chaos in the world; the gods are too busy bashing each other to help us meager humans. Being the god of wine, grape harvesting, partying, and fertility, I have a conspiracy theory on why Dionysus was designated as the god of fun. His dad, Zeus, made Cronus regurgitate his siblings (Dionysus' aunts and uncles) at a party, using wine. Since, Dionysus came out of Zeus' body, he became the god of wine and partying. Totally makes sense, right? On a serious note,

Dionysus preferred to skip the drama and travel the world with his followers rather than being propped up on a pedestal on Mount Olympus. Honestly, cultivating grapes and being the first to discover and teach winemaking to humans and partying without a care in the world is much more fulfilling and fun. Come to think of it, who wants to deal with #SCANDAL and all of the gods dramas? Hestia is definitely the smart one out of the bunch; there is a saying, "older is wiser" and Hestia is the eldest of all the Olympian gods. Oh no, does that mean my sister and parents are wiser than me? That's ludicrous!!!!!!!

CHAPTER 7: APOLLO IS SIZZLING HOT (NO, LITERALLY)

Apollo is a very, how can I say this...he's a very sizzling hot god. He's sizzling hot, because he's the god of the sun at least that's his main purpose. He's also the god of prophecy, music, poetry, archery, healing, and the plague. Don't ask me why these Greek gods have so many jobs. I think they should unionize and get better working conditions and employ more gods like me; as mentioned before, I'll take the role of god of wealth/MOOLAH! Okay, less activism and trying to find a gig for myself and back to Apollo. Apollo is the son of Zeus and Leto, goddess of modesty and womanly demure. Unlike Zeus' other relationships, Leto, Zeus and Hera's cousin, became pregnant before Hera and Zeus got married, but gave birth after they wed. In other words, Leto was Hera's first victim when it came to Zeus' relationships with other goddesses/women...the start of #SCANDAL.

Now to more pleasant facts, Apollo has a twin sister, Artemis, who is identical in personality to him. PSYCHE! She's the polar opposite of him, where he's the god of the sun; she's the goddess of the moon. They also both act like sun and moon, yin and yang, polar opposites, apples and oranges, cats and dogs, have I driven my point across? Continuing, Apollo is very social and forthright, while on the other hand, Artemis is a loner and introverted. Okay, this is getting boring, let's move on to the #SCANDAL part.

By now you well know Hera, Zeus' first wife, made Zeus swear that she would be his one and only wife. Zeus made the promise, but he broke his promise to Hera, time and time again, as evident in previous chapters. After her wedding, Hera learned that Leto was pregnant with Zeus' children and Hera was so outraged that she threw a tantrum like a little baby, that's a simile (I'm not letting Hera read this book, with her temper, I'd be in hot water. She may even send the boogey-monster, Lamia, after me). Back to Hera having a tantrum like a little baby, this is what went down; when Apollo and Artemis were in their mother's womb, yes goddess also give birth, Hera set out a python monster to chase Leto. Yes, a snake python, but not just any python; a big one that talked and could devour you in one bite. Hera also cursed Leto not to find solid ground on earth. Hera thought she was smart, she thought she knew the answer to 1+1 was

2.0000001; yeah, she was close, but unfortunately for her, she needed to be spot on. In short, Hera's plan almost worked, until Zeus soiled her pants, I mean, soiled her plans. Zeus created an island called Delos where Leto gave birth to Apollo and Artemis. I bet Leto is going to go straight to Starbucks to get her caffeine fix from giving birth to twins and order a Grande Cinnamon Shortbread Cappuccino.

Hera was not the only one heartbroken though, Apollo is said to be a very handsome god, but he doesn't have the best luck in love. Here is the breakdown of his most epic failed love story, I like to label it "Baby Man, Dude's Revenge," and yes, you heard me right, and you'll see why. Apollo thought Eros / Cupid / Baby Man's, bow & arrow was babyish. He rudely commented "What's that?" With an attitude, making cheeky gestures. Eros thought, let's show you baby powder, I mean baby power, DUN, DUN, DUUUN! Eros made Apollo fall in love with a mortal woman named Daphne, but Eros made it so Daphne didn't desire Apollo. Apollo kept trying to persuade her to marry him; eventually she got so fed up, she prayed to Zeus to turn her into a tree. Can you imagine, praying to your future father-in-law to turn you into a tree and having to "T" pose for the rest of eternity all so his son can leave you alone? Zeus granted her wish and turned Daphne into a Laurel tree. Apollo cut off one of the branches of the tree...true love, decapitating your loved one, no better way to remember her, and he made the

Laurel tree, his sacred tree. In conclusion, Apollo is a sizzling hot, conceited, vain, and overworked god with no luck in the love department.

CHAPTER 8: ARTEMIS HAS A GIRLS-ONLY CLUB

Alright, how do I explain Artemis? She's a very "moony" god. No not moody, although she could be easily agitated; "moony" in that she's hidden most of the time and not "moony" meaning she's in love and unaware of her surroundings. In fact, other than Hestia, Artemis is the only other major Olympian goddess who hasn't and will never bear a child. The two are called the maiden goddesses; Athena is also considered one, but she has children, so I don't know why she's considered a maiden. Artemis is the maiden goddess; the goddess of the moon, forest, hill, the hunt, and archery (in conjunction with her twin brother, Apollo). When she was born, she left her mother's, Leto's, arms and scurried to her father Zeus' lap and announced "Dada? Can I have a bow and arrow and a bunch of hunters who will follow me around the woods, never get married and kill stuff with me?" Zeus

Greek Gods for Kids

then replied by saying, "Sure sweetie! Anything for my little warrior princess goddess" (mature babies back then, huh?).

You're probably thinking: how does Artemis survive? I know right - without any fast food chains in the forest - the thought just haunts me. Oh, you want to be one of her followers? Well, if you're a boy, you're out of luck, as boys are not allowed to join her "GIRLS-ONLY CLUB". GIRL POWER; oh no, I sound just like my mom... I'm going to have nightmares with my mom singing "Girls Just Wanna Have Fun," an 80's song by Cyndi Lauper; case in point, my mom is almost as old as Artemis. As I was explaining, Artemis recruits only female hunters, these girls must swear to never marry, have children or have any romantic encounters (for one, it doesn't bother me, girls have cooties anyway). Back to the female hunters, once you are initiated in Artemis' hunting club and you're caught in a lie, you get eternally punished...just kidding you just get kicked out of the cooties club; sorry, I meant to say "GIRLS-ONLY CLUB". Now doesn't the THB club sound good right about now? Refer to Hades chapter if you don't know what I'm talking about. Being part of Artemis' club is not all bad; one perk of being one of Artemis' hunters is you never age while being in the club. Come to think of it, my mom wants to join too, she says, "Never grow old, you won't have to deal with any husband or kid responsibilities...sign me up!"

With all that said, I feel Artemis may be a hypocrite, because there are rumors that she loved Orion, the son of Poseidon and Euryale (daughter of Minos, the king of Crete). When Artemis was with her nymphs walking around her neighborhood (caves, forests and trees), she noticed Orion in the woods. The nymphs immediately attacked, but before Orion could slay them, Artemis turned the nymphs into constellations in the sky to protect them. Artemis and Orion grew to be friends, but her brother Apollo was worried Artemis would break her maidenhood vow and marry Orion. Apollo, being the overprotective older brother by 2 seconds, came up with an evil plan; while, Orion was walking on the shoreline, Apollo challenged Artemis to shoot that "random person" trotting on the shoreline. Their conversation probably went like this: "'Hey Artemis.' 'What?' 'I triple-dog head dare you to shoot the random person over there.'" Yes, I announced triple-dog head instead of a plain dare because I was just at the THB club and thought of Hades' three headed dog, Cerberus. I bet Artemis would love to hunt him. Anyway, since gods don't care about most of us mortals, Artemis just shrugged and executed the dare. When she checked to see who she shot, she realized it was Orion. Apollo squealed, "Congratulations, you completed the dare successfully and killed your boyfriend!" Artemis, after having some choice words for Apollo, placed Orion in the sky and made him into a constellation. At least, Orion won't have to be tortured listening to "Girls Just Wanna Have Fun" and hopefully he escaped from having cooties because if he didn't, he will have cooties for the rest of eternity; no literally, he's a constellation! As you may know, Orion, is one of the most famous constellations of all time and it's all because of Apollo and Artemis. Case in point, Artemis is extremely impulsive and fierce, just like a wild wolf howling under a full moon.

CHAPTER 9: ATHENA BREAKS THE HEADLINE (THAT IS ZEUS' HEADLINE)

By the title of this chapter, you're probably thinking this will be a boring news report with the word "headline" blaring and just as boring as your first impression of this book but wait! This is a different kind of headline. By "headline", I mean Athena was born out of Zeus' head. You're now thinking: how did she get out of his head, oh that's easy to explain...she just pounded on Zeus' forehead (a.k.a. his headline) just like a baby would kick in their mom's stomach; just like I did, before I was born. My mom tells me stories of how I would karate kick her so hard in the womb that she would lose her breath and fall to her knees while tears streamed down her scarlet cheeks! Wait, should I be proud of that? Well you can't blame me; I was born a week early and one ounce shy of 10 pounds. I needed

Greek Gods for Kids

to **GET OUT**!!!! My mom says, I was given the name "**Shaya**" from being one ounce **shy** of 10 pounds and the **hiya** sound made when doing a karate kick. Well, I guess "Shaya" is better than what my sister named me before I was born: Bing-Bing. Anyway, let's talk about how it all started and what led up to Athena leaping out of Zeus' head. Just a warning, in this story, Zeus acts exactly like his cannibalistic father, Cronus…like father, like son.

The story of Cronus tells of a prophecy that one of his kids would take over his throne, so he ate his children to prevent the prophecy from happening. The story of how Athena was created started when Zeus swallowed his current wife, Metis, because he heard a prophecy that she would have 2 children: one powerful and one that will take over his throne as the "king of gods." Zeus swallowed Metis, by turning her into a fly. Yes, you heard me right, a fly; the only thing I could think is "Eeew, how could he eat a fly?" but I guess he's not the only one; there is a children's book called "The Woman Who Swallowed a Fly," I wonder if that book was inspired by Zeus swallowing Metis? Anyhow, as a fly, Metis flew inside Zeus' head and gave birth to a child, not the one that would take over Zeus' throne, but the "powerful one." By saying this, I imagine a baby in a diaper with a superhero costume equipped with a cape babbling "Pow-Pow Super-baby". However, the real story is, Metis created Athena in Zeus' head and Athena leaped out fully grown. I still think a "Pow-Pow Superbaby" with a cape, would have been epic.

Prior to leaping out of Zeus' head, Metis turned Athena into the goddess of wisdom, reason, war, arts, and crafts. Athena eventually got bored of being cooped up in Zeus' head just as I got bored in my mom's womb, and she started pounding from inside his head. In one version, as a result of the pounding, Zeus got massive headaches and nonchalantly asked his son Hephaestus to split his head open and get out whatever was inside. Sorry Zeus, but that's not how it works. Anyway, Hephaestus, the god of blacksmiths, happily obliged and cracked his father's head wide open with a hammer...sophisticated. When Zeus' head was split open, Athena charged out fully grown and in full body armor. She became one of the major Olympian goddesses by showing off her wisdom and kung-fu skills- HIYA! Yet in another version, legend has it that Hephaestus was born solely by Hera as retribution for Zeus giving birth to Athena. Irrespective, Athena leaped out of Zeus' headline and became his favorite child; probably because he knew she wouldn't dethrone him.

Now I'm going to tell you my favorite story about Athena, which involves her destroying an arrogant mortal woman named Arachne. Arachne was the most popular weaver in all of Greece, she could weave anything! You may think Athena, being the goddess of arts and crafts, was jealous,

Greek Gods for Kids

but she's not envious like her father, Zeus. Athena is very level headed, cool tempered, humble, and doesn't like to initiate feuds; however, all bets are off if she's challenged, and challenged she was when Arachne made a public statement challenging Athena in a weaving contest. So naturally, Athena came to destroy Arachne. While all of Arachne's fans surrounded her, one exclaimed "This can only be a gift from Athena, the protector of the weavers." Arachne yelled, "This is not a gift from Athena! All the work here is a gift of my own. I must say, I 100% believe my work is much better than Athena's." Apparently, Arachne wasn't aware that Athena was the goddess of (1) wisdom (2) reason (3) war and (4) arts and crafts; all critical elements to destroy a challenger.

Being the goddess of wisdom and reason, as a first ditch effort, Athena disguised herself as an old lady and approached Arachne by flattering and praising her as a very talented young lady, but to challenge Athena, she must be out of her mind. Arachne ranted, "I'm better than her and I'm only speaking the truth." At this time, Athena took off her goddess of wisdom and reason hat and put on her goddess of war, arts, and crafts hat and in disgust spouted, "You think you're better than a goddess? Well let's have a face off." Athena then transformed out of the disguised grandma mode who was about to pull Arachne's ear so viciously, her ear would've fallen off...sounds like my friend's grandma. Anyway, once transformed, Arachne and Athena had a weaving contest and that's when I lost interest... but I have to remind myself to wait, until the end of the story, there's an alluring fact that will make some of you yell "COOL!" Athena weaved a picture of her beating Poseidon in a battle to earn the city that she named Athens; while, Arachne wove a picture of Zeus kidnapping Princess Europa and deceiving her by pretending to be a white bull. Don't even try to imagine a god saying "Moo" while attempting to kidnap someone. Oh no, I know, I'm now going to have nightmares about it! This is obviously a sign of how evil gods and goddesses can be.

Long story short, Arachne won the contest, and Athena wondered how did this reckless, impulsive, rude, and vain mortal girl beat me in a weaving contest? Athena then snickered at Arachne, "You like weaving, eh?" And for all you kids, reading this, name an insect that weaves...exactly, the tarantula that sleeps next to you. Wait, you don't have a tarantula that sleeps next to you? Well, that's a pity. Anyway, Arachne was turned into a spider and that's how spiders were created. Now, if you don't like spiders; remember, Spiderman wouldn't have been created without spiders (mind blowing) and Charlotte's Web, well bye-bye to that too! Lesson learned, as a mortal, never say you're better than the goddess of war or have the audacity to challenge her!

CHAPTER 10: APHRODITE IS SNOW WHITE 2.0

You can't not love Aphrodite (did you like the double negative sentence, I used?). No, I'm serious, it's literally impossible, being the goddess of love and beauty, she has a belt that makes you see the most gorgeous human being you could ever dream of. In ice cream terms, it's like a grilled banana split with hot fudge, caramel sauce, and all the candy toppings you can ever want and of course with whipped cream and a cherry on top.

Detoured again; seriously now, let's talk about how Aphrodite was created. Brace yourself as this could not be made up, even I am not that creative. She was created by the white foam produced by Uranus' cut off body parts thrown into the sea by his son Cronus. Uranus was the god of the sky/heaven before his son Cronus mutilated him, and that's how Cronus became king of the Titans and where he heard the prophecy that one of his children would eventually dethrone him...ONE WORD...#KARMA. And yes; I know, Uranus sounds like something you'd rather not think or talk about. Back to the point, when Cronus threw Uranus' body parts into the ocean, the ichor/ blood of immortal god mixed with the saltwater and it created prancing pegasi, the furies, torturing spirits, and finally the most boring being, the goddess of love and beauty, Aphrodite. Hey, don't judge I'm a 10-year-old boy. You know, "girls have cooties".

One day, when Aphrodite was floating through the sea, singing "Do re mi fa so la ti do", she stumbled upon a deserted island. As she walked across the sandy shore, flowers sprouted at her feet. It was basically Disney's "Snow White" in Greek mythology. That same day, the three seasons, Spring, Fall, and Summer, (as Winter wasn't created yet, as explained in the Hades chapter), decided to meet on the island to discuss what seasonal aisle Rice Krispie treats would be located in. Upon arrival, they laid eyes on the beautiful goddess, Aphrodite, (a.k.a. Snow White 2.0). Instead of discussing Rice Krispies destiny, (R.I.P Rice Krispies), they focused their undivided attention on Aphrodite. The seasons discussed taking Aphrodite to Mount Olympus to meet the Olympian gods. The seasons held a fashion show to see what Aphrodite would choose to wear to Mount Olympus. Spring featured a bunny costume; Fall presented a zombie ensemble, and lastly, Summer fashioned a glimmering white silky dress. Guess which one Snow White 2.0 chose? Exactly, she chose the bunny costume. Just kidding, she obviously chose the glimmering white silky dress; boring...I think the bunny or zombie options would have made a better first impression when meeting the gods.

Aphrodite finally arrived at Mount Olympus and strolled into the main hall to meet the "major" gods and goddesses. As expected, all the goddesses thought "I hate her," while all the gods started staring, drooling, and tripping over their words. It went down something like this; all the gods were yelling "I would love to marry you." "NO! I would love to marry you." "NO! I would love to marry you." Hephaestus, the god of fire and blacksmith, felt rejected because he was absolutely hideous and knew he would never win Aphrodite over with his looks.

Meanwhile, the goddesses were fed up with the drama and they feverishly looked around for a solution. When the gods finally simmered down for a split second, Hera seized the moment and beckoned, "SILENCE! I believe I know the right god to marry this beautiful goddess. I believe it's my son..." the god of war, Ares, exclaimed "YES! IT'S ME, I'M HER SON!" But Hera ignored Ares and proceeded by announcing, "Hephaestus is the right match for this splendid goddess and I believe my husband will support my decision." Zeus then snapped out of his staring trance of Aphrodite and supported his wife by grumbling "What? Oh yeah, I think that's a great idea." The other gods weren't as angry as they would've been if Hera decided on one of the other major gods to be Aphrodite's husband, as Hephaestus was hideous and pitied by all. In short, by Hephaestus marrying Aphrodite, it prevented a war of the gods fighting for Aphrodite's hand in marriage...see it pays to be the underdog. When Hephaestus heard his name, he was so startled that he stumbled out of his throne. He then proclaimed to Aphrodite, "I might not be the most handsome god ever, but I promise, I'll be the best husband you could ever wish for." Aphrodite tried looking revolted and beautiful all at the same time, which is an oxymoron, catch 22, and impossible, all wrapped in one. After they wed, they lived happily ever after, just like Snow White 1.0, PSYCHE! Obviously, it wouldn't turn out well; what were you expecting, a fairy tale? This is Greek mythology, not a Disney movie. Hello, wake up and smell the coffee, candy or whatever wakes you up.

Since Hephaestus was the god of fire and blacksmiths, every day he would schlep to his forge and work on creating weapons. While Hephaestus was slaving away, Aphrodite had the perfect opportunity to spend her day with Ares. Hephaestus eventually figured out what was happening behind his back and sought retribution. Hephaestus set his plan in motion by adopting an adorable doggy from the rescue shelter named Toby (okay so I'm using

Greek Gods for Kids

the name Toby because my dog's name is Toby and he's the cutest pug on the face of the planet) for them to fall in love with and then...I'm getting way too carried away with this. Let's start over, Hephaestus wanted revenge, so one day when he "left" for the forge as usual and he trudged down Mount Olympus, but on this specific day, he turned right around and headed home. Low and behold, he caught Aphrodite and Ares together, (if you were paying attention, you would know, Ares and Hephaestus are brothers, remember almost all gods and goddesses are related...family drama). Since Hephaestus had previously set up a net to trap the love birds, as Aphrodite and Ares were like "WEEEEEE-EEEE, WE'RE HAVING SO MUCH FUN!" Hephaestus trapped them in an unbreakable golden net. He then gathered all the gods and goddesses to humiliate them and display them trapped in the golden net. They all belly laughed hard, like really hard, and for a few millenniums it went viral on **Godstagram**, **Godbook** and **Godchat**. So, the moral of this chapter is Aphrodite sucks.

CHAPTER 11: HEPHAESTUS PUTS HIS MOM IN TIMEOUT

Hephaestus is the god of fire, blacksmiths, stone masonry, and the art of sculpture. After Hephaestus seeks reprisal on his wife, Aphrodite, and brother, Ares, in the infamous unbreakable golden net scandal, featured in the previous chapter, Hephaestus divorces Aphrodite and marries and raises children with Aglaea, the Greek goddess of beauty, splendor, glory, magnificence, and adornment. What's ironic is Hephaestus was born lame and classified as the only "ugly god" amongst flawless beautiful gods, but somehow, he managed to marry the goddess of love (Aphrodite) and the goddess of beauty (Aglaea); how did he pull that off? Next time you see an unattractive man with a beautiful woman, don't use the obvious cliché "Beauty and the Beast" use a more sophisticated and coded phrase like "he pulled a Hephaestus."

Hephaestus was so hideous, legend has it that

his mom, Hera, was so disgusted and ashamed of having a lame, deformed and ugly child and afraid of being mocked by the other gods that she threw Hephaestus from the top of Mount Olympus in hopes to never see him again, but Hephaestus managed to make his way back up the mountain and claim his residence at Mount Olympus as one of the major gods. There are conflicting stories about Hephaestus' lineage (specifically, whether Zeus was his dad or not) and if he was ever a major Olympian...go figure. The version of mythology I would like to recap has a good explanation as to why Hephaestus was so ugly... it was because his parents were Hera and Hera... yes, in this version, he had no dad, but he was created solely by Hera. Legend has it, Hera wanted to get back at Zeus for giving birth to Athena, so she created a baby by herself; I know it confuses me too.

After being discarded by his mom like last night's trash, Hephaestus made his way back up Mount Olympus and he told all the gods his story of survival and, it seemed that in lieu of seeking retribution, he graciously presented his mom, Hera, with an alluring golden throne as thanks for creating him. All the gods had just heard of how Hera tried to get rid of her own son and thought "Oh, how sweet that he's gifted his mom with an extravagant throne; it's totally not a trap," and they all praised Hephaestus for the beautiful gesture and present, symbolizing his gratitude of being created by Hera.

Obviously, Hephaestus had an ulterior motive and wasn't truly present to echo, "Thank you mom for creating me" rather, he was there to spout, "You threw me off a mountain as an infant, because I was deformed and ugly and now you will regret being regurgitated by Cronus."

Obviously the gods were so occupied on Godbook for the past 17 hours prior to Hephaestus ploy, losing their souls in their early released phones, because they didn't notice anything amiss as Hephaestus spread something on the seat called glue, causing Hera to be eternally stuck on the magnificent throne. Just kidding, Hephaestus didn't place glue on the seat of the throne, but he did secure many delicate cords that self-tie around the person (Hera) who sat down on the throne. Oh, did I forget to mention, only Hephaestus could see or remove the cords? #PAYBACK!!!!! After a while of listening to Hera complaining, nagging and ranting; for their peace of mind, the gods pleaded with Hephaestus to set Hera free to no avail. They even offered Hephaestus a home on Mount Olympus, befriending him on Godbook and giving him a 10% off coupon at Dominos, but he still didn't budge. Until Dionysus gave him an abundance of wine (playbook from Zeus), putting him in a jolly mood and causing him to finally free Hera. Since, the gods had to keep their word in fear of what Hephaestus may do to them, Hephaestus got a 10% discount at Domino's, had the most followers on Godbook, and earned a seat on Mount Olympus, as one of the major Olympians. The highlight, of course, was the 10% coupon from Dominos.

Although Hephaestus was linked to beautiful goddesses and a mother and brother he loathed, he was best known for his clever inventions, refined weaponry, beautiful craftsmanship, and the ability to withstand any amount of heat without combusting. Legend has it, Hephaestus' forge/workshop was situated under a volcano and that his work often caused volcanic eruptions just like the onion volcano eruptions featured at Benihana. Hephaestus is known to have crafted Athena's shield, Eros/ Cupid's arrows, and Achilles' armor. In addition to making the immortals weapons, he also crafted their dwellings and furnishings evident by the throne he made for his mommy dearest, Hera. All in all, Hephaestus is a peace-loving god; although, his mother, brother and wife betrayed him, he only embarrassed them and detained them for a time being; think of it as a "time out" rather than a beating. Trust me, if it was any other god/goddess, there would be Tartarus to pay.

CHAPTER 12: IS THE WORD NIGHTMARES, ORIGINATED FROM ARES?

Ares is the most hated god of all time; that's why there is no "Treat Ares Better Club," unless the Spartans, an ancient Greek warrior society, created the website, but if they attempted to use a computer, they'd probably just stab it with their swords, because they would have to watch a 10 minute ad and wouldn't know how to press skip. I once met a Spartan, the only words I heard blaring in my ears, were "fight, blood, death, fight, blood, death"…oh yeah and did I mention "fight, blood and death"?

Except for the Spartans, most people despise Ares, because of his conceited and self-righteous attitude and his eternal love for war. On the other hand, the masses believe one should be humble and

Greek Gods for Kids

they desire "peace, love and happiness"; yes, there is still hippie blood soaring through our veins. People also dislike Ares because he's impulsive and insensitive, stabbing a bunch of people with his sword when they merely scored a touchdown on him. Yeah, I don't blame people for being terrified of him. I may have a theory as to why Ares is so vicious, ruthless, and callous: his mom and dad are Hera and Zeus. His mom attempted to kill every mortal and banish every goddess Zeus had a relationship with and his dad, Zeus, trapped Demeter in a hole and ate Metis, Athena's mom, to avoid being dethroned.

There are numerous, embarrassing, stories about Ares such as, Athena beating him in a battle with a mere rock and Ares being intertwined in a golden net with Aphrodite, as described in the Aphrodite chapter. As humiliating and hilarious as these stories may be, we're sticking with another epic Ares story. Okay, this story features Hercules, one of the greatest demigods later turned into a god, but during this encounter he was still a demigod. Since Hercules was the son of Zeus and a mortal woman named Alcmene, (a.k.a. Ares' brother from another mother)...I know, Disney got it wrong, as Hercules' mom was NOT Hera, as depicted in the Hercules' Disney movie, but that's not the first time Disney got it wrong, as I should be a Disney princess, but I'm not; isn't that crazy? WHAT? I can't be a Disney princess because I'm not a girl...minor details.

Anyway, Hercules was driven insane by Hera's

actions (a.k.a. **3Rs**), causing him to kill his wife and children. To be absolved of his sins, he went to the oracle at Delphi and was told that he needs to serve 12 years under the Greek king of Mycenae, Eurystheus, resulting in Hercules performing 12 impossible challenges called labors. Two of the feats involved Hercules stealing items from Ares' children. The first child of Ares that Hercules' stole from was Hippolyta. I know, funny name right, but what happened to her was no laughing matter; SHE WAS THE QUEEN OF THE AMAZONS. No, not the company Amazon where everything is a click away, but the group of girl warriors that run around the Amazon rainforest and slaughter men. No fair, another "Girls-Only Club," come on Greek mythology, we need some "Boys-Only Club" action...other than the boy bathrooms, which are always grimy, filthy and smelly. Okay, I just lost my appetite; now back to the Amazons. Hercules managed to attain Hippolyta's magical golden belt for Eurystheus' daughter and without Amazon Prime to replace the belt, Hippolyta was dethroned as the queen of the Amazons. Well, it didn't quite work out that way; actually, Hippolyta was killed due to Hera's interference once again. For another one of his impossible labors, Hercules had killed Ares' son, Eurytion's, and stolen his red oxen. These events had Ares irritated. Ares' is such a mama's boy; all this was caused by his mom Hera. Why is he mad at Hercules...IT'S NOT HIS FAULT! Remember, Hercules was forced to do the 12 labors due to Hera driving him to kill his own fam-

Greek Gods for Kids

ily, so don't side with Ares just yet.

Although Ares was irritated about Hercules stealing from Hippolyta and Eurytion, he wasn't mad enough to rip Hercules' guts from the inside out. All that changed when Hercules completed his 12 impossible labors and Apollo "needed his help." This is how it all began, Ares' son, Kyknos, who was known for ambushing pilgrims and stealing offerings on their way to the oracle (a medium through whom a prophecy is revealed), truly infuriated Apollo, the god of prophecy, as he desired safe travels for the pilgrims. Apollo enlisted Hercules assistance to "deal with" Kyknos. "APOLLO FOR GOD'S SAKE, YOU ARE A GOD; DEAL WITH HIM YOURSELF!" Long story short, Apollo won the strong arming and sent Hercules on his way to "take care of it". The truth of the matter was that Apollo was scared Ares would kill him if he interfered with Kyknos' mischievous ways; even though, Apollo is immortal and can't die, being a god and all. Hercules' interference in Kyknos' mischievous ways made Ares lose his marbles and go ballistic, challenging Hercules to a fight. Hercules proudly accepted the challenge. When the two clashed, you can say they were equal in strength, Hercules being the most powerful demigod of all time and having the protection of Athena behind him was truly a force to be reckoned with. In the end, Hercules wounded Ares and made him run home crying to mommy. Let's put it this way: that's basically saying, you're an adult and a little 4-year-old beats you up and sends you running the other direction. The story of "Hercules' and Ares' Battle" is one of the most epic stories defaming Ares. It serves Ares right; Hercules' gave Ares *night*m*ARES*, as Ares has given *night*m*ARES* to endless families by causing wars. Come to think of it, is the word nightmares originated from night + Ares? I mean, Ares does make people go night-night forever and the word *night*m*ARES*, starts with "night" and ends in "Ares". Thereby, proving my point as to why no one has and no one will initiate a "Treat Ares Better Club".

CHAPTER 13: HERMES, THE TURTLE AND THE COW

Hermes truly lives up to his name, being the god of trade, thieves, and travel; not to mention, being notorious for his extreme mischievousness. Even as a newborn he could outwit Apollo; although handsome, Apollo was never the god of intelligence. Hermes was the son of Zeus and Maia, the daughter of Atlas. To protect Hermes from the wrath of Hera, Zeus turned Hermes into a caveman; it was 500 BC, but that's beside the point. By saying "turned" him into a "caveman", I mean he threw Hermes in a cave with his mom Maia where Hermes remained in a baby cradle for the rest of eternity... just kidding. I know; I know, Zeus still hasn't learned his lesson of Hera's attempts to murder every single kid Zeus bore with someone else. I think the electricity bolts have permanently fried Zeus' brain.

Having nothing to do and being cooped up in a

cave, baby Hermes waited for the right opportunity to sneak out and take matters into his own hands. At 4-days old, Hermes craved steak and decided he was going to find a way to eat Apollo's sacred cows. In addition to being hungry, Hermes thought it would be a fun adventure; honestly, mature babies back then times 2. Though it doesn't start with 4-day Hermes licking the aromatic filet mignon juice off his stubby fingers, it will soon get to that point. As a 4-day baby, Hermes saw a turtle and he yelled "STOP! WHERE ARE YOU GOING?" Little did this turtle know that it was soon going to be, how do I say this in a pleasant way? HIS FINAL DAY ON EARTH! Hermes told the turtle, "I shall follow you! We will be best friends!" But the turtle, thought of all the phantasmagorical effects of being BFFs with an unsupervised, 4-day old baby god; so, he kept walking. When he went to get a refreshing sip of water, Hermes announced his intentions out loud, "So you don't want to be my friend?" Hermes then sighed, "Oh well, you shall sing more sweetly than the birds" and proceeded to karate chop the turtle's head off. I wonder if this is how the French invented the guillotine?

Now, you're probably thinking: how does a decapitated turtle sing? Read and you shall find out... Hermes hollowed out the turtle's shell and grabbed the intestines and stretched them across the shell, making it into a sling to carry the turtle. He also used the intestines as cords. When Hermes played his new instrument, it played/sang better than the songbirds. Long story short, Hermes wasn't lying to the decapitated turtle that he would sing sweeter than the birds. Proud of his accomplishments, 4-day old baby Hermes went stumbling around the forest, playing his turtle instrument while birds and deer were doing ballet behind him and caroling "LALALALA!" Hermes officially became Snow White 3.0, after Disney's Snow White and Aphrodite, Snow White 2.0. He raced through forests, past the shoreline, down the red carpet, through Sleeping Beauty's castle, and woke her up; yeah, his decapitated turtle sang that well.

Hermes then got bored of meeting princesses, so he set out for some steak. By that I mean, he approached Apollo's sacred cows and was planning to eat them; Apollo totally won't be furious and try to throw you into Tartarus. Anyhow, Hermes causally trotted up the plateaus, past the hills and through the rivers, nearing Apollo's cows. Hermes thought "One of the gods with eternal power won't mind if I only take a few of his cows," emphasizing *a few*. Hermes finally got to the oxen, sat down, and he stared and stared and stared: "I think I'm just going to take a few dozen, hmm this steak better taste superb, being Apollo's sacred cattle and all!" To make sure Apollo wouldn't be able to trace his tracks, baby Hermes tied twigs to his stubby little feet and to the oxen's legs. Hermes thought, "I would love to eat all this steak in my cradle, while I play my decapitated turtle." Please, don't ask me why Hermes has a mansion baby crib. Hermes went through the hills and saw a farmer staring at him in awe. Hermes then stared him down and definitively announced, "You will not tell anyone I was here!" The farmer just stared at him, surprised by seeing a 4-day old baby with a decapitated turtle and Apollo's sacred cows following him. Hermes just kept walking and then murmured, "Weirdo…" Once Hermes ate an entire cow, he regretted it. He didn't regret eating too much; I know I regret eating too much, when I dine at Fogo De Chao, my all-time favorite, all-you-can eat Brazilian steakhouse. Hermes regret wasn't with overeating, rather his regret had to do with what Apollo may do to him. Yeah, see that mom; you call me impulsive, look at Hermes. My mom rolled her eyes and mumbled, "He's 4-days old, you're 10-years-old, so I expect more of you." "True…"

Just as expected, Apollo was livid. He immediately initiated a search to find his missing sacred cows. His optimism diminished as he searched everywhere and asked everyone about his cattle's whereabouts to no avail. Until, Apollo stumbled across the "weirdo" farmer and asked him if he knew where his cattle were. At first the farmer refused to talk, because he was threatened not to say anything by a 4-day old baby. Apollo then promised the "weirdo" a splendid harvest and the farmer was so excited that he disobeyed the 4-day old baby's

Greek Gods for Kids

commands. How could he do such a thing? The man sold out Hermes and divulged the entire story to Apollo...by that, he made a time machine, traveled to the future, grabbed this book, WITHOUT PAYING and read this chapter. Oh, and by the way, old farmer dude, there's a fee for doing that! Apollo now knew who stole his sacred cattle, Toby my pug. Just kidding, Apollo knew that Hermes did this unthinkable act.

With a vengeance, Apollo set out for Hermes' cave, featuring a mansion sized baby cradle. When Apollo arrived, he demanded for the safe return of his cattle. Hermes first covered his eyes and ears and said "Goo-goo ga-ga?" Supposedly, meaning he was a harmless baby that was incapable of stealing the great Apollo's cattle. Apollo then attempted to coax Hermes into telling him where his cattle were by offering Hermes a godly lollipop, while Hermes attempted to hypnotize Apollo with his big googly eyes and baby lisp. Baby Hermes chanted, , "Trust in me," as done by Kaa, the snake from "The Jungle Book," but when that attempt failed too, Apollo was fuming and threatened Hermes by hollering, "I'll throw you in Tartarus, if it's the last thing I do!" Apollo then frantically ran home crying to daddy and wailed, "My 4-day old half-brother (a.k.a. your newborn, cave baby), Hermes, just stole my cattle and he won't give them back." That's equivalent to a 32-year-old man, calling 9-1-1 because his 2-year-old infant took his collectible vintage toy train and would not give it back. Zeus then set a trial to determine if Hermes is guilty or innocent...what happened to speaking with your kids and resolving the conflict at home?

Hermes of course brought his decapitated turtle to the trial, because everyone needs their trusty decapitated turtle companion in court, right? Apollo and Hermes argued and blabbered, and when it was discovered that Hermes ate Apollo's sacred cattle (I wonder if Apollo influenced the Hindu religion, revering cows as sacred), the gods sentenced baby Hermes to Tartarus. Fortunately for Hermes, Apollo had a passion for music, so as Hermes was about to be escorted to Tartarus, he brought out his trustworthy decapitated turtle and started playing it and singing along. Hermes then pleaded, "If you don't send me to Tartarus, I will give you custody of my...." In that one moment, Hermes thought of the one thing that described him, and the word he thought of was a liar. Although his spelling wasn't great, he found the name of his instrument, a lyre; at least he tried to spell it. Apollo couldn't refuse Hermes offer, Apollo agreed to spare Hermes from Tartarus, and earned custody of the liar's lyre. The moral of the chapter is NEVER MESS WITH BABIES. Dating back to the story of Eros, come to think of it, Apollo has really bad blood with babies: first, Eros and now, baby Hermes. In conclusion, Hermes is the god of trade, thieves, and travel, because he thinks on his toes and can outwit anyone.

CHAPTER 14: THE OLYMPIAN GODS' INTERTWINED FAMILY

If you were paying attention and doing the math, you would know I covered 14 Olympian gods/goddesses in this book. The truth of the matter is; at different times, different gods were considered as part of the "Twelve Olympians". It's like the game telephone, as the stories were told and retold over generations the stories were heard, remembered and/or interpreted differently. I hate to break it to you, but those family stories your grandparents and parents told you are probably nothing like what actually occurred. Like the stories of your grandparents walking barefoot in rags for 10 miles in the snow each way to get to and from school... let's just say, they may have added a zero after the one and they were probably sporting the latest snow jacket and boots fashioned with a trendy hat, scarf, and mittens.

One fact that has not been exaggerated is the notion that the greatest Greek gods / goddesses were referred to as the "Twelve Olympians" or "Olympian Gods". All Olympian gods/goddesses had palaces on Mount Olympus where they congregate to discuss important matters. Except for Hades, who dwelled in the underground and Poseidon who mostly resided in his palace under the sea; the remaining Olympians lived on Mount Olympus year-round, unless they were vacationing or traveling for work.

Beware; if you hear another version of the stories discussed in this book just remember "Telephone". Other than conflicting Greek mythology stories, another confusing matter about the Greek gods are their relations to one another. If you recall, Uranus and Gaia were Cronus' parents and six of the Olympians grandparents including Zeus, Hades, Poseidon, Demeter, Hera, and Hestia and the great grandparents of the remaining Olympians (all who were Zeus' children) with the exception of Aphrodite who was created from Uranus' body parts, discarded into the sea, by Cronus, his son. Talk about family drama; mom really, compared to the Olympian Gods, our Thanksgiving dinners are divine.

In conclusion, I hope you enjoyed my book, found it entertaining, and learned a thing or two about Greek mythology. If you enjoyed my book, please tell your friends, family, and neighbors about it. If you didn't enjoy it, then keep it to yourself and revert to your electronics or whatever makes you happy. Well hey, at least it wasn't a complete waste; it got your parents off your back for a little while.

ABOUT THE AUTHOR

Shaya Dadmehr is proud to share "Greek Gods for Kids" with you. Shaya is an outgoing, witty, curious, and at times sarcastic 10-year-old boy who lives in Southern California with his exuberant puppy, adoring older sister and loving parents. Shaya thoroughly enjoys sports such as basketball, football and martial arts and has the travel bug for new destinations, so he can learn and experience various cultures and lifestyles. Shaya has a fondness for reading, writing, history, arithmetic and sports statistics. Shaya's favorite place to write is in bed, late at night, when he should be sleeping. Shaya's favorite topics to write about are personal narratives, current events, fantasy and mythology. When writing, Shaya's advice is, "if you get writer's block, take a break, go do something new, fun and/or relaxing and when an idea pops into your head, race toward your computer, or piece of paper, and write feverishly." Most importantly, his advice is to read an array of books and articles whenever time allows; for when you read, it opens your mind and imagination to new and exciting events and worlds; undoubtedly, making you a better author and a more interesting person, as a whole. Shaya dedicates this book to his family and teachers, for making him a better writer and pushing him to his limits.

Thank you for reading my book :)
-Shaya Dadmehr

Printed in Great Britain
by Amazon